MY Propeller PLANE

To: Camryn & Meghan
Sweet dreams,
Jillian L. Nowlan

BY JILLIAN L. NOWLAN

ILLUSTRATED BY KATE WHITMORE

My Propeller Plane by Jillian L. Nowlan
Illustrated by Kate Whitmore

ISBN: 9780615446417
Library of Congress Catalog Number: 2011901906

Edited by Jill Ronsley, SUN Editing & Book Design
www.suneditwrite.com

Printed and bound in the USA

Published by Cloud 9 Children's Books, Inc.
P.O.Box 78813 Charlotte, North Carolina 28271.

Book Design by Kate Whitmore
www.katewhitmoreart.com

For my parents, Paul and Mary Lamoureux. Thank you for making my childhood a very, very happy one.

--Jillian

For Drew, my husband and my dearest friend.

--Kate

Flying in my propeller plane
Over waving fields of grain.
Dipping, diving, loop de loop,

Upside down

— alley-oop!

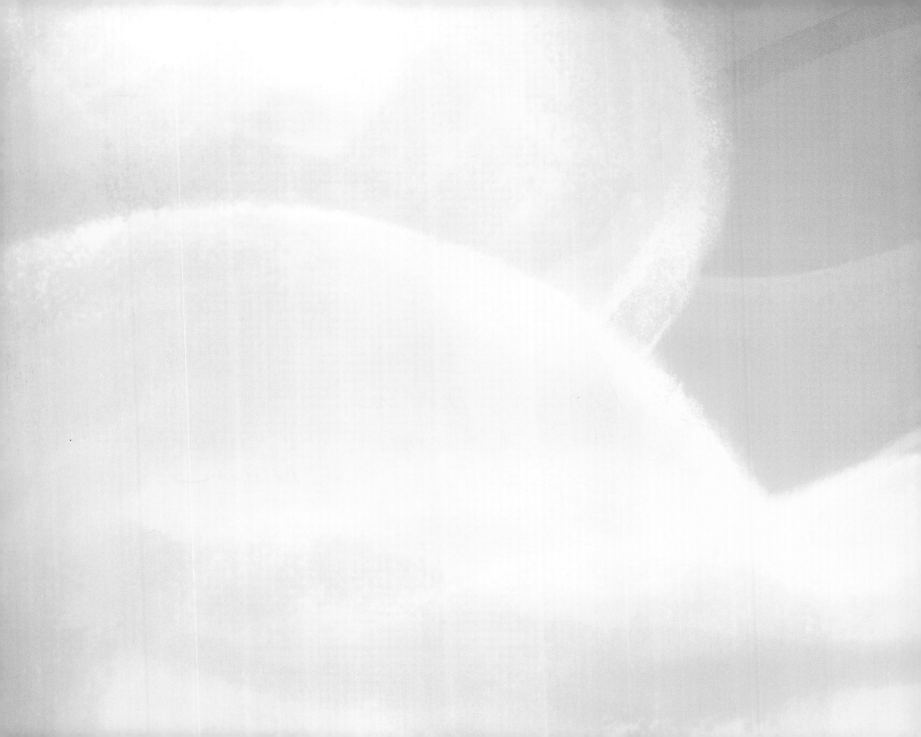

Through the clouds, soft and fluffy;
Marshmallowy, light and puffy.

Up the mountains, tall and steep;
Snowy-capped, icy deep.

Over the river, blue and long;

Sparkly, bubbly, rushing strong.

Down a valley, lush and green;

Leafy landscapes, petals gleam.

Under the moon, bright and clear,
With a smile from ear to ear.

In all directions my plane will fly,
Across a vast and endless sky.

It's getting late — now turn around
And travel back, homeward bound.

Good night moon, bright and clear;
Time for a hug and kiss, my dear.

Good night valley, lush and green;
Time for pj's, teeth are clean.

Good night river, blue and long;

Time to sing a lullaby song.

Good night mountains, tall and steep;
Time to close my eyes and sleep.

Good night clouds, soft and fluffy;
Time to hold my favorite lovey.

On my pillow I lay my head
And dream of soaring from my bed.

Flying in my propeller plane
Over waving fields of grain.
Dipping, diving, loop de loop,

Upside down

— alley-oop!